INDIAN TRAILS
PUBLIC LIBRARY DISTRICT
WHEELING, ILLINOIS 60090
847-459-4100
www.indiantrailslibrary.org

DEMCO

WordBooks
Libros de Palabras

House

La Casa

by Mary Berendes • illustrated by Kathleen Petelinsek

Published in the United States of America by The Child's World®
1980 Lookout Drive • Mankato, MN 56003-1705
800-599-READ • www.childsworld.com

Acknowledgments
The Child's World®: Mary Berendes, Publishing Director
The Design Lab: Kathleen Petelinsek, Design and Page Production

Language Adviser: Ariel Strichartz

Library of Congress Cataloging-in-Publication Data
Berendes, Mary.
 House = La casa / by Mary Berendes ; illustrated by Kathleen Petelinsek.
  p. cm. — (Wordbooks = Libros de palabras)
 ISBN 978-1-59296-992-0 (library bound : alk. paper)
 1. Dwellings—Terminology—Juvenile literature. 2. Picture dictionaries,
English—Juvenile literature. 3. Picture dictionaries, English—Juvenile
literature. I. Petelinsek, Kathleen. II. Title. III. Title: Casa. IV. Series.
 GT172.B47 2008
 392.3'6014—dc22   2007046567

house
la casa

chimney
la chimenea

roof
el tejado

garage
el garaje

windows
las ventanas

garage door
el portón del garaje

door
la puerta

driveway
el camino de entrada

porch
el porche

sidewalk
la acera

mailbox
el buzón

street
la calle

3

light
la luz

tools
las herramientas

shovel
la pala

hose
la manguera

tool bench
la mesa para
herramientas

car
el coche

driveway
el camino
de entrada

4

garage
el garaje

thermometer
el termómetro

bike
la bicicleta

lawn mower
la cortacésped

yard
el jardín

trees
los árboles

playset
el equipo de
juego infantil

doghouse
la perrera

REX

dog
el perro

fence
la valla

front yard
el jardín delantero

6

shrubs
los arbustos

backyard
el jardín
trasero

garden
el jardín

grass
la hierba

flowers
las flores

7

doorway
la entrada

cabinet
el armario

stove
la cocina

pot
la olla

hallway
el pasillo

oven
el horno

cat
el gato

clock
el reloj

kitchen
la cocina

refrigerator
el refrigerador

sink
el fregadero

TO DO:
dishes
dust
groceries

list
la lista

microwave
el microondas

ice maker
el dispensador
de hielo

dishwasher
el lavavajillas

rug
el tapete

floor
el suelo

chandelier
la araña

napkin
la servilleta

table
la mesa

plate
el plato

chair
la silla

glasses
los vasos

dining room
el comedor

mirror
el espejo

spoon
la cuchara

knife
el cuchillo

cups
las tazas

saucer
el platillo

fork
el tenedor

living room
el salón

fireplace
la chimenea

television
la televisión

painting
el cuadro

fire
el fuego

pillows
los cojines

couch
el sofá

bowl
el cuenco

table
la mesita

curtains
las cortinas

plant
la planta

armchair
el sillón

lamp
la lámpara

carpet
la alfombra

13

telephone
el teléfono

computer
la computadora

pencils
los lápices

mouse
el ratón

keyboard
el teclado

desk
el escritorio

chair
la silla

office
la oficina

shelves
los estantes

printer
la impresora

books
los libros

file cabinet
el archivador

15

lamp
la lámpara

pillow
la almohada

teddy bear
el osito de
peluche

blanket
la manta

nightstand
la mesilla

bed
la cama

bedroom
el dormitorio

ceiling fan
el ventilador
de techo

dresser
el tocador

alarm clock
el despertador

knob
el tirador

drawer
el cajón

shower curtain
la cortina de baño

shower
la ducha

shampoo
el champú

rubber duck
el pato de caucho

washcloth
la toallita

towel
la toalla

bathtub
la bañera

scale
la báscula

18

bathroom
el baño

mirror
el espejo

faucet
el grifo

toothbrushes
los cepillos de dientes

toothpaste
la pasta
dentífrica

toilet paper
el papel
higiénico

sink
el lavabo

soap
el jabón

toilet
el inodoro

slippers
las zapatillas

closet
el armario

door
la puerta

belt
el cinturón

raincoat
el impermeable

jacket
la chaqueta

pants
los pantalones

doorknob
el pomo

boots
las botas

shoes
los zapatos

20

hat
el sombrero

purse
el bolso

hook
el gancho

hangers
las perchas

dress
el vestido

sweaters
los suéteres

shirts
las camisas

tie
la corbata

sandals
las sandalias

flip-flops
las chancletas

shoes
los zapatos

laundry room
el lavadero

detergent
el detergente

shelf
el estante

dryer
la secadora

washer
la lavadora

clothes
la ropa

basket
la cesta

flowers
las flores

ironing board
la tabla de
planchar

iron
la plancha

plug
el enchufe

dog bowls
los cuencos para
comida de perro

cord
el cordón

REX

word list
lista de palabras

alarm clock el despertador	**file cabinet** el archivador	**plug** el enchufe
armchair el sillón	**fire** el fuego	**porch** el porche
backyard el jardín trasero	**fireplace** la chimenea	**pot** la olla
basket la cesta	**flip-flops** las chancletas	**printer** la impresora
bathroom el baño	**floor** el suelo	**purse** el bolso
bathtub la bañera	**flowers** las flores	**raincoat** el impermeable
bed la cama	**fork** el tenedor	**refrigerator** el refrigerador
bedroom el dormitorio	**front yard** el jardín delantero	**roof** el tejado
belt el cinturón	**garage** el garaje	**rubber duck** el pato de caucho
bike la bicicleta	**garage door** el portón del garaje	**rug** el tapete
blanket la manta	**garden** el jardín	**sandals** las sandalias
books los libros	**glasses** los vasos	**saucer** el platillo
boots las botas	**grass** la hierba	**scale** la báscula
bowl el cuenco	**hallway** el pasillo	**shampoo** el champú
boxes las cajas	**hangers** las perchas	**shelves** los estantes
cabinet el armario	**hat** el sombrero	**shirts** las camisas
car el coche	**hook** el gancho	**shoes** los zapatos
carpet la alfombra	**hose** la manguera	**shovel** la pala
cat el gato	**house** la casa	**shower** la ducha
ceiling fan el ventilador de techo	**ice maker** el dispensador de hielo	**shower curtain** la cortina de baño
chair la silla		**shrubs** los arbustos
chandelier la araña	**iron** la plancha	**sidewalk** la acera
chimney la chimenea	**ironing board** la tabla de planchar	**sink (bathroom)** el lavabo
clock el reloj		**sink (kitchen)** el fregadero
closet el armario	**jacket** la chaqueta	**slippers** las zapatillas
clothes la ropa	**keyboard** el teclado	**soap** el jabón
computer la computadora	**kitchen** la cocina	**spoon** la cuchara
cord el cordón	**knife** el cuchillo	**stove** la cocina
couch el sofá	**knob** el tirador	**street** la calle
cups las tazas	**lamp** la lámpara	**sweaters** los suéteres
curtains las cortinas	**laundry room** el lavadero	**table** la mesa
desk el escritorio	**lawn mower** la cortacésped	**table (small)** la mesita
detergent el detergente	**light** la luz	**teddy bear** el osito de peluche
dining room el comedor	**list** la lista	**telephone** el teléfono
dishwasher el lavavajillas	**living room** el salón	**television** la televisión
dog el perro	**mailbox** el buzón	**thermometer** el termómetro
dog bowls los cuencos para comida de perro	**microwave** el microondas	**tie** la corbata
	mirror el espejo	**toilet** el inodoro
doghouse la perrera	**mouse** el ratón	**toilet paper** el papel higiénico
door la puerta	**napkin** la servilleta	**tool bench** la mesa para herramientas
doorknob el pomo	**nightstand** la mesilla	
doorway la entrada	**office** la oficina	**tools** las herramientas
drawer el cajón	**oven** el horno	**toothbrushes** los cepillos de dientes
dress el vestido	**painting** el cuadro	**toothpaste** la pasta dentífrica
dresser el tocador	**pants** los pantalones	**towel** la toalla
driveway el camino de entrada	**pencils** los lápices	**trees** los árboles
	pillow (bed) la almohada	**washcloth** la toallita
dryer la secadora	**pillows (throw)** los cojines	**washer** la lavadora
faucet el grifo	**plant** la planta	**windows** las ventanas
fence la valla	**plate** el plato	**yard** el jardín
	playset el equipo de juego infantil	